CHURRO AND THE Magician

Gastón Caba

ETCH
Houghton Mifflin Harcourt
Boston New York

First U.S. edition

Etch is an imprint of Houghton Mifflin Harcourt Publishing Company.

hmhbooks.com

The illustrations in this book were done digitally.
The text was set in Toronto Subway.
Cover design by Kaitlin Yang

Library of Congress Cataloging-in-Publication Data is on file.
ISBN: 978-0-358-46773-1 hardcover
ISBN: 978-0-358-46775-5 paperback

Manufactured in China
SCP 10 9 8 7 6 5 4 3 2 1
4500830771

1373
MAIL

ESC1

MAGIC
SHOW

CLAP!
CLAP!
CLAP!
CLAP!

AGIC
HOW
TAXI
223
TAXI
223
TAXI
223
TAXI
223

CRUNCH!
CRUNCH!
NOM!

1
2
3

WHOOSH!!!

CHOO-
CHOO

CHOO-CHOO

3
2
1
RB

TV

TV

2
4

RB
1
TV
TV

PSST...
PSST...

FINISH
CHAN'S